wisenheimer wednesday

Look for more of
doug & mike's Strange Kid Chronicles:

#1 *Mighty Monday Madness*

#2 *Tunafish Tuesday*

Coming soon to a bookstore near you:

#4 *Just Thursday*

. . . but don't look for anything else because we
haven't finished Friday yet. Duh.

DOUG & MIKE'S

STRANGE KID

CHRONICLES

wisenheimer
wednesday

AN

APPLE

PAPERBACK

SCHOLASTIC INC.
New York Toronto London Auckland Sydney

No part of this publication may be reproduced in whole or in part, or stored in a retrieval system, or transmitted in any form or by any means, electronic, mechanical, photocopying, recording, or otherwise, without written permission of the publisher. For information regarding permission, write to Scholastic Inc., 555 Broadway, New York, NY 10012.

ISBN 0-590-05956-4

12 11 10 9 8 7 6 5 4 3 2 1   8 9/9 0 1 2 3/0

Printed in the U.S.A.
First Scholastic printing, January 1998

dedicated to my mom & dad.

When Douglas isn't making children's books he's making video games and movies. Douglas does not have a Caldecott. Douglas owns three cats named Simon, Waffle, and Mr. Black. Changing the litterbox is one of his chores.

dedicated to my brother Matt.

Mike had a dog, but it died. Then he got another dog, named Sugar. The dog stays at his dad's house, because having two kids is enough for now. Mike is happy he doesn't have to clean up the doggy poop anymore. He stays busy making pictures for books and video game boxes

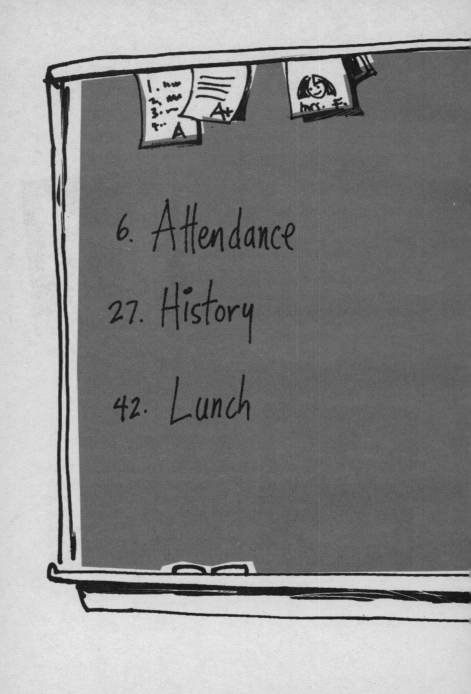

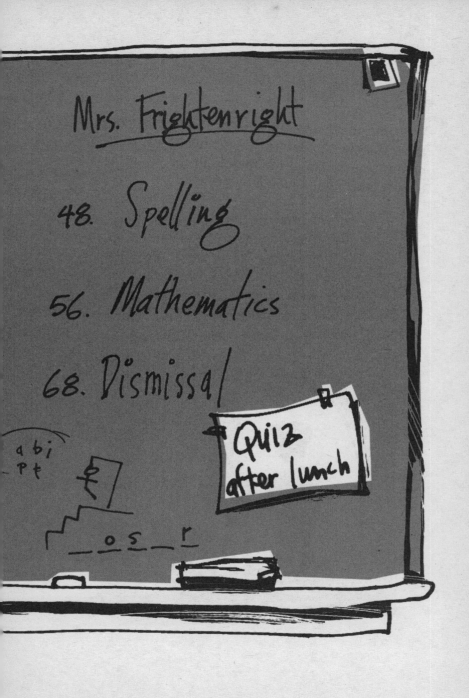

Hey, Man!

Welcome to Wednesday, one of the funkiest days of the school week. Before we make our way to school on this smack-dab-in-the-middle-of-the-week day, let us first take a good look at ourselves.

How different do you think you are? Different enough to be a student in Mrs. Frightenright's class? Now, when I mean different, I'm not referring to those of you who wear giant floppy green boots, have a set of ears that kinda stick out too far, or wear a cute little mole on your cheek.

No, I'm talking **way out** like those two kids over there . . . the one who is half-fish and half-boy and the hairy one who could easily be mistaken for a shaggy carpet. Their differences will do nicely. Now, come along with Mikey Mold and Doug O'Dork as they stroll to Mrs. Frightenright's class.

Pretty cool . . . Very tempting . . . I dare you not to turn the page.

I DARE YOU!

Boy, that was easy. We didn't even have to
DOUBLE DOG DARE YOU!

BeST FRieNDS

Mikey Mold and Doug O'Dork opened their lunch bags as they walked along a curb. Doug said, "Aw, man! My mom gave me a pimiento-loaf sandwich. Who in the

1

world invented a loaf of meat that contains green olives?!"

Mikey Mold looked into his lunch bag and answered, "Probably the same goon that invented my stupid chocolate cake!"

"Yeah, man, stupid chocola – " Doug stopped and looked at Mikey's lunch bag. "What do you mean STUPID chocolate cake?"

Mikey Mold said, "I mean that I'm sick and tired of my dad always giving me a giant piece of chocolate cake covered in thick chocolaty

frosting for lunch every day of the week."

Doug licked his lips. "Uh, Mikey?"

"What?" Mikey answered.

Doug asked, "You want to trade your chocolate cake for my pimiento-loaf sandwich?"

Mikey jumped at the offer. "Are you crazy?! Of course I would!"

Doug held out his lunch bag to Mikey. "Here you go, pal. I really kind of wanted my pimiento-loaf sandwich, but I'll sacrifice for you. I'll eat your chocolate cake as a favor."

Mikey's face got real serious. "You know, Doug O'Dork, you're such a great friend that I wouldn't dream of making you eat my yucky chocolate cake!"

Doug started to sweat. "No, really, pal, I don't mind!"

Mikey said, "No way! I won't let you do this. I'll choke down this awful piece of chocolate cake all by myself!"

Doug grabbed Mikey by his arm. "Mikey!

GIVE ME THE CHOCOLATE CAKE!"

"Don't have a cow!" Mikey said as they switched bags.

Doug reached into his new lunch bag and pulled out the . . .

His face turned bright red as he screamed,

"THIS IS NOT A PIECE OF CAKE! THIS IS A ROTTEN OLD DEAD FISH!"

Mikey, of course, had run into Mrs. Frightenright's class, leaving Doug alone on the sidewalk holding his new stinky lunch.

ATTENDANCE

Mrs. Frightenright began taking attendance as a cricket started chirping in the corner. Principal Prickly-Pear oozed into the class like the stench from a skunk. Prickly-Pear stood over Mrs. Frightenright and said, "Mrs. Frightenright, you seem to have an insect problem."

Jared the Pig whispered to

Big Mouth Moira, "Principal Prickly-Pear seems to have a body odor problem!" Big Mouth Moira laughed so hard that she snorted! Prickly-Pear whirled around to see who was

laughing. The principal's glaring eyes caught Moira's. She became so scared that her smile quickly turned into a frown of chattering teeth.

"Does SOMEBODY think SOMETHING is funny?!" Prickly-Pear asked, staring directly at Moira and Jared. Jared tried with all his might not to look at the principal's eyes.

But the terrified pig could feel Prickly-Pear's glare cutting right through him. Finally, Jared covered his squinting eyes with his hooves and cried out, "I can't take it anymore!

It was Moira!"

Moira yelled, "Why, Jared! You no-good snitch!"

Jared sobbed like a baby. "She laughed because I said you had a body odor problem!"

Everyone burst into laughter! Even Mrs. Frightenright had to smile. Principal Prickly-Pear didn't find this amusing, of course.

"So, Moira, you think it's funny that Jared

said that I have a body odor problem?!", Principal Prickly-Pear screamed.

Moira, nervously shaking, blurted, "N-n-no, Principal. I wasn't laughing at that. I was laughing that Jared would think that you had a problem with body odor when it is much clearer that you have a serious dandruff problem!"

The classroom erupted with laughter again. Weird Ellis laughed so hard that a giant vein popped out of his forehead. Principal Prickly-Pear turned to Mrs. Frightenright and screamed,

"You will learn to control this unruly classroom right down to the last bug, or I will transfer you to another school by the end of the week!"

The kids fell silent. Only the chirp of the cricket could be heard. Principal Prickly-Pear scowled one last time, started to hiccup, and then stormed out of the classroom with dandruff flakes drifting close behind.

Mrs. Frightenright saw that the strange kids were pretty scared, so she said, "Don't pay any attention to that mean old man. We won't let him scare us!"

Mrs. Frightenright then finished taking attendance. And once again, Chirp! Chirp! Chirp! went the cricket as the whole class tried to ignore the songs. Big Mouth Moira looked down at the corner where the chirping was coming from and scowled. Moira put her fingers in her ears and said, "This stupid cricket is making such a racket I can't hear myself think."

Weird Ellis said, "Hey, Moira, we can't hear ourselves think, either, over your big mouth!"

Moira yelled back at Ellis, "Weirdo with the Weird Eye!"

"Mouth the size of my garage!" Ellis returned.

Mrs. Frightenright said, "Stop with the insults! I will see what the cricket situation is!" She went over to the corner and got down on her hands and knees. Mrs. Frightenright put her head down against the tile floor and squinted, trying to see under the art cupboard.

"Gosh, lady, that darn cricket will be a distraction for the rest of the day to us all!"

Mrs. Frightenright looked up and asked, "Who said that?"

"Who said what?" Truman asked.

"Who just called me 'Lady'?" she said.

"I did," the little voice replied.

Mrs. Frightenright looked up, down, and all around.

The little voice repeated, "Hey! Lady! Down here!"

Mrs. Frightenright followed the voice, eagerly looking down at the tile in front of her.

"Here!" the voice said.

Finally, still on her hands and knees, Mrs. Frightenright saw the tiniest kid in a tiny crevice.

Mrs. Frightenright announced to the rest of the class, "There's a tiny boy named Byron over here on the floor!"

The class gasped.

Mrs. Frightenright grabbed a magnifying glass and held it up to Byron so she could see what he looked like. She was shocked! He looked just like a toddler she once knew named Byron. Except, of course, back then it was impossible to miss that toddler because Byron was 6 feet 9 inches tall when he was two years old. In fact, she remembered that when Byron was born, he was even taller than that! Byron topped all world records by being the tallest baby ever born, measuring 7 feet 3 inches tall.

As you might imagine, it was not an easy birth for the mother. And it was very hard to buy clothes for him. Byron had to wear twin bed-sheets for diapers. That's right, his parents actually wanted him to wet the sheets!

Byron's parents were afraid that if he was this big now, what would he be like when he got older? One evening Byron's parents went outside, feeling completely desperate because Byron had just rolled over and flattened the family poodle.

They looked up at the dark sky to wish on a star, chanting:

"Star light,
Star bright,
First star we've seen tonight.
We wish we may
We wish we might
Have a boy of smaller height."

And boy, oh boy, did their wish come true. In fact, instead of Byron growing up, he grew down! It happened that the older he got, the smaller he got.

Presently, Byron looked as old as most of the other kids his age but in a teenier and tinier version. His miniature size wasn't so bad at first. In fact, it had its benefits. When Byron's friends brought their action toys over to his house, he not only could play with them, but could also play *in* them. After all, he fit perfectly in the little vehicles, riding and shooting their blasters. And when his friends lost money down the drain, they'd lower Byron down on a pencil for him to retrieve it.

However, the advantages were limited. Mostly, Byron was lonely. And the smaller he got, the more trouble his friends had finding

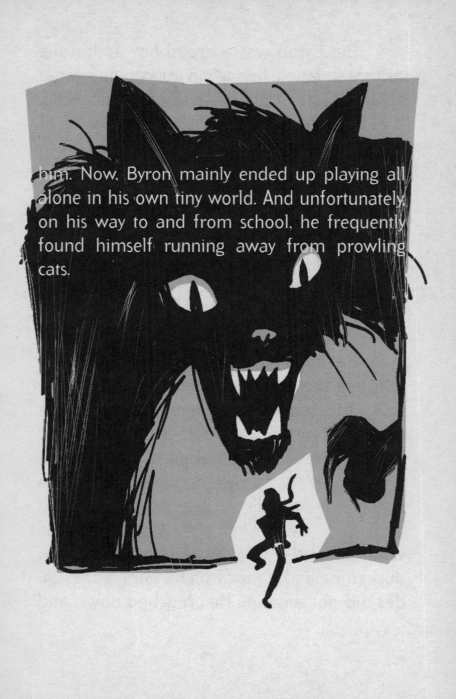

him. Now, Byron mainly ended up playing all alone in his own tiny world. And unfortunately, on his way to and from school, he frequently found himself running away from prowling cats.

But Byron was a proud boy and in the current situation, he saw an opportunity to put his small size to good use. Byron announced, "I've been in your class since the beginning of the school year. You have taught me so much that I'd like to show you my gratitude by hunting down that cricket. I'll put a stop to his racket!"

Mrs. Frightenright thanked Byron. "I would appreciate it if you could make that cricket be quiet. I can't teach with that irritating noise!"

Byron said, "No problem, Mrs. F!"

He slipped into the crack in the wall and followed the chirp-chirp-chirping of the cricket. As Byron crawled deep into the walls of the classroom, he was careful to avoid the deadly heating pipes that ran throughout them.

Byron saw something moving off in the distance. It was hairy, its legs were gangly and each one was packed tightly with varicose veins. It was a big, honkin' spider! Byron ducked behind a jar of paint, hoping the spider did not see him. He crouched down and froze. After a few minutes, Byron peeked around the corner of the jar and noticed that the spider was no longer there.

Clean getaway, Byron thought. But Byron seemed to have missed the fact that the huge, ugly spider had cleverly tiptoed right up behind him. The spider was so excited. He opened his mouth wide and stuck his fangs

straight out, ready to take a huge bite of the little guy.

Then it happened. The spider's bean-and-broccoli sandwich caught up with him. And he let out a big burp. That's right, a spider burp! It was loud and smelly.

Startled, Byron fell backward, waving his hand in front of his nose and saying, "P.U. Someone cut the cheese!" Byron, bumping right into the spider, felt a fang against his shoulder. This was Byron's cue to run as fast as his short little legs could take him. But the spider's longer legs started to gain on him.

Luckily, Byron ran past a bottle of glue. He quickly tipped the bottle of glue over and the sticky liquid poured across the floor. The spider walked up to the puddle of glue and stopped. "Hey, little boy!" Mr. Spider began. "Do you taste good? Because I'm going to find out! I see this glop of glue and I'm not going to walk into your trap!"

The spider then realized he was talking to himself. Byron was no longer anywhere to be seen. That's because Byron gave Mr. Spider a taste of his own medicine. This time it was

Byron who sneaked up right behind Mr. Spider! Byron kicked the spider in the butt, which pushed the bug into the glue face first! The more the spider tried to get away the more stuck he became! Byron finally got on with his journey to find that blasted cricket!

Byron followed his ears to a tiny hole in one of the boards under the sink. Byron wriggled into the hole, and spread out before him was a tiny living room. It was quite love-ly. There was a fireplace, beanbag chair, orange bead curtains, and bookshelves. Then his eye caught a glimpse of a needle, leaning against a thimble in the corner. Byron walked over to the needle and grabbed it. Stabbing at the air with the needle, Byron pretended to hold a sword. "I'll show that cricket when I skewer his giz-zard!" Byron yelled in his best pirate voice.

Clutching his sword, Byron proudly walked through the living room and found the kitchen. He saw a slice of apple sitting on a plate with many tiny bites taken out of it. Byron then looked up from the plate as he heard a "chirp." And there it was . . . the crick-et . . . sitting in a chair, reading the newspaper, having his morning coffee, and chirping. Byron noticed that the cricket was not rubbing his legs together to chirp like he had thought

crickets did. Instead, the cricket was rubbing his wings together to make the squeaky song.

Byron jumped on a matchbox next to the cricket and said, "Prepare to meet your Maker!" The cricket was so startled by Byron's sudden burst into the room that he jumped out of his chair and whacked his head on the low ceiling. The cricket sat on the ground, rubbing his head.

"You realize that I am quite angry with you!" the cricket said.

"Get a weapon, you lousy coward!" Byron yelled, swinging the needle to and fro.

The cricket stopped rubbing his head and looked at Byron's legs. "You make so much noise for such a tiny little boy!" the cricket said.

"Did I hear you call me TINY?!" Byron screamed.

The cricket grabbed a toothpick and whipped it in the air, making a great whooshing sound! The tiny fighters clashed weapons. At first it looked as though Byron would easily beat the cricket, but the cricket was just letting Byron show off a bit. And once Byron had his time, the cricket waved his toothpick around like a seasoned professional. Byron began to sweat as he realized he was about to lose the swordfight in a big way. As Byron lay there with the cricket's foot on his chest and the toothpick waving in the air, Byron started to cry, "And all I wanted to do was something nice for Mrs. Frightenright!"

The cricket low-ered his toothpick and watched the boy weep. "Continue," the cricket demanded.

"I promised her that I would make you stop chirping," he sobbed.

The cricket said, "Is that all you wanted? You should have just asked!"

That's all? Byron thought as he wiped the cricket's footprint off his chest. The cricket shook hands with Byron, forming a strong bond and a deep respect for each other.

Byron came back to the class and Mrs. Frightenright thanked him again. Mrs. Frightenright said, "A nonchirping cricket is a happy, quiet cricket."

She placed a tiny pink eraser on her desk and said, "Byron, here is your new seat, right at the front of our class!" Byron smiled and hid a chunk of Mrs. Frightenright's apple in his pocket to share with the cricket later that day.

HISTORY

Mrs. Frightenright announced that it was time for history. The students pulled out their social studies books. Gary of the 6th Dimension slumped down in his seat, dreading whatever the history assignment would be. You see, Gary of the 6th Dimension was terrible

27

at history. For instance, the other students knew that George Washington was our first president of the United States, but Gary thought the president was a dolphin named Bill.

Mrs. Frightenright handed out the assignment. "Write a poem about the Pilgrims and the *Mayflower*. You can make it funny or serious, but it is due before lunch."

Gary of the 6th Dimension wished he was in the 6th Dimension so he could disappear and avoid writing a poem about the

Pil-grins and the Mayfowler. While Mrs. Frightenright was writing at the chalkboard, Gary of the 6th Dimension leaned over and whispered to Byron, "I'm going on a little trip. I'll be in the Sixth Dimension. Then Mrs. Frightenright won't see me and she won't notice if I don't turn in my history poem!"

Byron got excited. "Take me with you to the Sixth Dimension or I'll tell!"

Gary said those words that hit every kid right where it hurts: "Don't be a baby!"

"Sheesh! What a grouch," Byron said.

Then Gary of the 6th Dimension said the magic words:

"Hear my wish.
As I secretly mention.
Swim like a fish
Straight to the Sixth Dimension!"

Mrs. Frightenright turned around and asked, "Where did Gary of the Sixth Dimension go?" Byron decided not to tattle (because he knew what we know . . . that only babies tattle).

Gary looked around at the 6th Dimension. It wasn't at all like our dimension (the 3rd dimension). It was full of weird colors and strange beings called Mush-faces. Gary knew that if a Mush-face ever touched him, his face would instantly turn to mush. And because they were so mushy, they were fun to poke and therefore tempting to touch. Needless to say, staying away from Mush-faces was easier said than done.

Gary forgot how distressing the 6th Dimension could be, so he decided to say a rhyme that would bring him back to Mrs. Frightenright's class:

"Take me back
To Mrs. F's class.
I'll even eat the broccoli
That always gives me gas!"

But his rhyme backfired as Gary skipped through the **6th Dimension** and landed in the **7th Dimension**!

Mrs. Frightenright, with magnifying glass in hand, squatted down next to Byron and squinted so she could see him. "Byron," she asked, "have you seen Gary of the Sixth Dimension?"

Byron, the World's Smallest Kid, said, "I don't want to tattle on him and tell you that he went to the Sixth Dimension!"

Mrs. Frightenright was so shocked that she dropped her magnifying glass. Even Mrs. Frightenright knew that the 6th Dimension was a dangerous place for a boy.

I'll bet you're wondering what happened to Gary. Well, in the 7th Dimension, everything existed in piles of green goo that was full of microbes. Cool! One microbe (we think his name was Mike Roe) had seven eyes and ran around in circles like a lost dog. Very cool! It smiled and showed its big sharp teeth. Not so cool! The microbe looked back at Gary and said in rhyme:

"What are you looking at?
Boy whose head is full of fat!
You once were over there
And now you're over here.
If I were an actor,
I'd be Richard Gere."

Gary realized that these organisms liked to make funny rhymes. Gary of the 6th Dimension decided to take full advantage. He asked the green blob organism, "Hey, microbe! Since you can rhyme so well, can you think of a poem that might help me get back to the 3rd Dimension, where my school is?"

The microbe responded:

"Now? In a flash!
Like Johnny Cash.
My cornbread tastes
good mixed with hash."

Gary smiled and gave the microbe one limitation. "For my transportation magic to work, I need to find something that rhymes with 'Make me gigantic.'"

The microbe thought for a second, and then said:

"A boat was filled with people
who came by Providence,
to land on Plymouth Rock.
I hope this makes some sense.
The words you're looking for
are 'Mayflower' and 'Atlantic.'
You'll find they rhyme quite well
with 'Make me gigantic'!"

Gary quickly wrote down the rhyme and repeated it five times. The words were potent and for every time he said his poem, he jumped to a dimension closer to the 3rd. . . .

Let's see, he went from the 7th to the 6th. . . .

Then he went from the 6th Dimension to the 5th. . . .

He didn't stay long at all in the 4th. . . .

Then, finally, he landed back in Mrs. Frightenright's class, which exists in the 3rd Dimension. Mrs. Frightenright saw Gary appear in class again and she hugged him and said, "I'm so glad you're with us, Gary!"

Gary, relieved he was back from the 7th Dimension, smiled and said, "A microbe helped me with my history poem!"

Gary handed his poem to Mrs. Frightenright. She read the poem and

said, "Class, I have an announcement to make! Gary was not only the first to turn in his history poem, but he also got an 'A'!"

And because of Gary's ability to travel to different dimensions, he frequented the 7th Dimension at every recess. To this day, nobody but Gary has seen the 7th Dimension (nobody else but the readers of this fine book, that is).

Mrs. Frightenright dismissed the class for lunch after collecting all of the poems on the *Mayflower*. As all the kids went to the cafeteria, Skeleton Joe left the class and hid in the bushes.

Skeleton Joe hated to go to lunch. He was, after all, a living skeleton. Because he was all bones, it didn't matter if he ate any food or not. He often ate rocks, wood, or whatever for the fun of it, since it all just fell out of his neck and onto the ground anyway. In fact, Skeleton Joe only drank milk to make sure his bones were always strong. He liked his milk rotten since it stuck to his ribs a lot more easily.

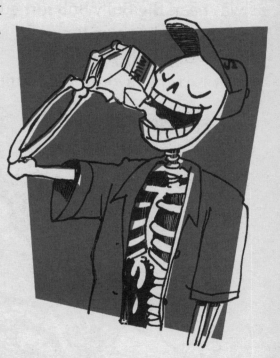

Skeleton Joe sat on a brick wall and sighed, "Whew! Nobody noticed that I'm hiding here. Now I won't have to deal with that evil Big Bully Bob, who's always bothering me."

Skeleton Joe noticed a swarm of flies suddenly whirling about him. At first he tried swatting a few, but there were just too many! Then he looked up. A swarm of flies could only mean one thing . . . that Big Bully Bob was near! Big Bully Bob turned the corner and sat on the brick wall next to Skeleton Joe.

Big Bully Bob belched. "Well, well, well! If it isn't my favorite pal, Skull-Boy!"

Skeleton Joe said, "I'm not your pal and my name is Skeleton Joe! Maybe if your brain was bigger than a microbe you might remember that!"

Big Bully Bob pulled out a thermos from his own lunch. He unscrewed the top and saw that it was filled with soup. Big Bully Bob held the thermos up to Skeleton Joe's mouth and said, "Take a swig! I wanna see it pour out of the bottom of your skull!"

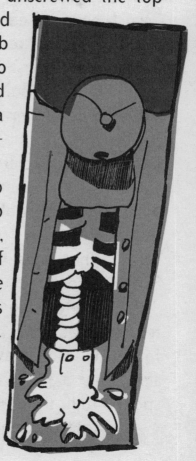

Big Bully Bob poured some of the soup into Skeleton Joe's mouth, and it went straight out of the bottom of his jaw! The soup splashed all over his ribs and down his pants. Bob pointed to Joe's soup-stained pants. "Looks like you wet yourself!"

Big Bully Bob looked at Skeleton Joe's lunch sack and said, "Now, gimme your lunch! Or I'll play your ribs like a xylophone!" Skeleton Joe surrendered his lunch.

Big Bully Bob pulled out the thermos from Skeleton Joe's lunch. Big Bully Bob said, "Watch now as I eat the lunch that your sweet old momma packed for you . . . and don't try to stop me!"

Big Bully Bob didn't care what was in Skeleton Joe's thermos. He just started drinking the contents. He threw the empty thermos back to poor Skeleton Joe, who just sat there watching. And then Skeleton Joe watched when Big Bully Bob buckled over, sick as a dog.

"What have you fed me?" Bob asked Skeleton Joe.

Skeleton Joe answered, "Oh, I forgot to tell you that I only drink rotten curdled milk for lunch. I don't have a stomach, so I can't get sick. Only a great fool would drink rotten, spoiled milk if he had a stomach!"

Skeleton Joe stepped away from Big

Bully Bob, who had a coagulated chuck of yellowish goo hanging from his lower lip. Big Bully Bob buckled over and barfed all the way to the school nurse. Nurse Terror gave him a tetanus shot in the rear.

SPELLING

After recess the kids lumbered back to class. Mrs. Frightenright announced, "Get out your spelling list from yesterday and review it. We are going to have a quiz!" Everyone got out their list and favorite lucky writing utensil. Weird Ellis had a pen with

a San Francisco cable car floating inside of it. Skeleton Joe had a pencil that was shaped like a bony finger. Wet Willis grumbled to himself, "B – A – D spells bad! Bad spelling test," and pulled out a plain old blue ballpoint pen. He was dreading this quiz. Wet Willis had not prepared for it like he should have, so he hoped someone who sat next to him had!

Wet Willis was half-boy and half-fish. He had green skin and gills instead of ears. His eyes were big and he could not blink, just like real fish. His lips were big and he had whiskers like a catfish. Willis could not be exposed to air, so he wore a special diving suit that allowed him to carry water with him everywhere he went. His helmet was a clear bubble, filled with water, which allowed him to see everything. Willis liked to blow bubbles

in his helmet, especially to music. In fact, if he heard a rock-and-roll song, he could blow bubbles in perfect time to the beat of the music.

Wet Willis propped his soggy body up in his chair, adjusting himself to a position where he could most easily peek at Gary of the 6th Dimension's spelling list. Gary saw what Wet Willis was doing and, covering up his paper with his arm, said, "Quit looking at my spelling list, you big cheat!"

Wet Willis finally decided to cheat by himself. He wrote the spelling words on the palm of his suit. He wrote as fast as he could with his ballpoint pen. About halfway  through the list, Mrs. Frightenright said, "Okay, class . . . put your spelling lists away. It is time to start the quiz!"

Wet Willis instantly wrote faster! He wasn't aware of the great amount of pressure with which he was writing, so his ballpoint pen speared through his suit and punctured the inner lining.

Water gushed from his hand, pouring everywhere. Big Mouth Moira yelled,

"TIDAL WAVE!"

Jared pulled out his surfboard and rode the giant wave.

Wet Willis looked down at his suit, watching the fountain of water squirt halfway across the classroom! The water shot into one of Mikey Mold's ears and went right out of his other ear!

Mrs. Frightenright looked at Wet Willis's helmet and saw the water draining out. Mrs. Frightenright was pretty scared. "Willis, you're

not breathing water anymore!!!"

Wet Willis did not know what to do,

"Someone help me! I'm drowning in air!"

Mrs. Frightenright responded, "Wet Willis, let me see the hole so we can clog it with something!"

Wet Willis didn't want her to see the spelling list written on his palm, so he clenched his fist tight. Mrs. Frightenright grabbed his hand and pried it open. She yelled, "Moira! Help me get Wet Willis to the faucet!"

Moira grabbed his head while Mrs. Frightenright grabbed Wet Willis's body and dragged him to the arts-and-crafts sink. Moira stuck the faucet into Willis's suit and was about to turn it on when Milo screamed, "Wait, Moira! That's the hot water!" Moira's hand was on the red handle, all right! Milo grabbed the blue handle and

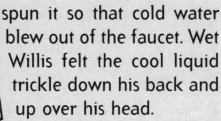

spun it so that cold water blew out of the faucet. Wet Willis felt the cool liquid trickle down his back and up over his head.

Willis could tell by the scowl on Mrs. Frightenright's face that she knew he had been cheating. Wet Willis was embarrassed, so he whispered to Mrs. Frightenright, "Please don't tell the class that I cheated. I won't cheat ever again. I promise!"

Mrs. Frightenright covered the hole and the ballpoint spelling list with duct tape until the water stopped pouring out. Mrs. Frightenright whispered back to Wet Willis, "I can cover this list with tape but I can't cover your wrongdoing. Just don't ever cheat in my class again, or the next time we will visit your parents!"

Wet Willis nodded. He was upset that he failed that spelling test, but he was glad that Mrs. Frightenright gave him another chance. The good news is that Wet Willis never cheated again!

MATHEMATICS

The custodial crew came into the room and mopped up the water mess. Mrs. Frightenright announced that it was time for math. The class was drilled on multiplication tables every day. She asked her students, "What is two times two?"

Most of the class raised their hands. Mrs. Frightenright picked Thing to answer. Thing grunted, "Two times two is four."

"Very good," Mrs. Frightenright said. "I am handing out a bunch of multiplication problems, and you have to finish as many as you can in five minutes."

"Big deal," Carlos said.

Mrs. Frightenright looked crossly at Carlos, responding, "The first student to finish will get a rare comb made of diamonds that I found on my trip to Africa last summer!"

Carlos yelled,

"Oh, my cow! Now that's what I call incentive!"

The whole class was suddenly very interested in multiplication. They sat straight and held their quivering pencils in hand. Mrs. Frightenright said, "On your mark, get set. . .

GO!"

The class was filled with the sound of pencils hitting paper. Other than the sound of intense scribbling, it was completely silent. Mrs. Frightenright enjoyed the peace and quiet and looked out the window, noticing a sparrow chirping happily.

One kid was thinking so hard that he stuck out his tongue and licked the sweat off his brow.

Another kid chewed the eraser off her pencil like a beaver.

Still another kid was nervously shedding.

This was Truman.

Truman was a boy covered with hair. Except for his hairless face, the rest of him looked like a shaggy carpet. And because he was so nervous about the quiz, some of his hair was falling out! Truman's desk quickly became covered in brown locks. Strands drifted everywhere.

Perhaps more than any of his classmates, Truman needed and wanted that comb. Clockboy pulled a piece of candy out of

his pocket. Before he could get it into his mouth it got smothered in Truman's airborne hair. Clockboy yelled, "I'm so discustipated!"

Mrs. Frightenright sneezed when some of Truman's hair floated past her nose. Truman quickly looked up, shouting "Bless you!" realizing it was his fault she was sneezing. "I'm sorry there is so much hair in the air, Mrs.

Frightenright. I can't help it," Truman explained.

Mrs. Frightenright wanted Truman to feel more comfortable in the classroom so she pulled out a big vacuum and turned it on. The noise blasted loudly, but at least Mrs. Frightenright was able to collect giant chunks of hair off her desk and the chalkboard.

The class looked up from their tests and saw Truman was obviously having a bad hair day. Big Mouth Moira got an idea! She pulled out a pair of scissors from her school supply box and screamed, "Let's give Truman a haircut!"

The vacuum was so loud that Mrs. Frightenright did not hear Moira's crazy plan. Moira jumped over a row of desks and started clipping Truman's shaggy coat. Moira hoped to be a hairdresser when she grew up, so she figured this would be great practice. (Not to be tried at home without adult supervision -- and also never run with scissors.) The class saw that Moira was having so much fun cutting Truman's hair that they dropped their pencils to help.

"When we cut off all of your hair, you'll look just like a **NORMAL** boy!" Moira said as the rest of the class joined in the cutting and styling of a potentially new hairdo for Truman.

Hair flew continuously all over the room. Mrs. Frightenright kept vacuuming the chalkboard and just when she thought she had it all cleaned up, it was covered with fur again! *Poor Truman*, Mrs. Frightenright thought. Moira finally pulled away a huge chunk of Truman's hair, this time from the roots, and saw that under all of that fur, Truman was covered with a layer of blue dragon scales!

Before long, the kids cut off all of Truman's hair. Now Truman had no hair at all, and he looked all slick and naked like a snake that just shed its skin.

Flying Vera yelled,

"Look at all of those blue scales! Truman is a total FREAK!"

The class made fun of poor Truman, whose scales were even stranger looking than his old shaggy fur. Truman realized that it was never worth it to try to please other kids with his looks.

Big Mouth Moira got another idea. "Hey, I wonder what's under all of those scales!"

The other kids were pretty curious.

Eustice guessed, "I'll bet there are even MORE scales!"

Weird Ellis hypothesized, "Perhaps he has normal boy skin underneath!"

Moira said, "There's really only one way to find out! . . . Let's peel off his scales!"

The kids started peeling off some of Truman's blue scales. Grant the Ant said, "This is funner than picking scabs!"

Jared the Pig said, "Yeah, but you can't eat scales!"

Mrs. Frightenright continued to vacuum the chalkboard when she noticed that she was no longer cleaning up hair anymore. She was now cleaning up scales! She thought that she must be going crazy seeing all of those blue scales, so she turned around and saw the class pulling at poor Truman's skin!

The only thing Mrs. Frightenright hated more than cheating was when a kid was picked on because he or she was different. Mrs. Frightenright turned off the vacuum and screamed, "Everyone get back to your seats immediately!" Moira hadn't seen Mrs. Frightenright this mad since the class locked Patrick the Catboy and Brandon the Mousekid in the broom closet together to see if they would fight!

By the time the kids got back in their seats, it was too late. All of Truman's scales had been pulled off. There he sat, all covered in hair again!

"Who'd have guessed that he had another layer of hair under all those scales?" Eyeball Smith said.

"Finished!" Truman said. The rest of the class turned

and saw Truman smiling.

"What?!" the rest of the class asked. They'd forgotten about the multiplication quiz! While they were busy picking at poor Truman, he was busy at work trying to earn that diamond-studded comb from Africa! Moira shouted, "Rip-off!"

Mrs. Frightenright giggled to herself and gave the comb to Truman. The comb was so valuable that by the time Truman graduated from high school, he was able to retire. He did not retire, though. He started a successful business as a Hollywood hairstylist! He became close friends with all of the famous movie stars of his time!

And whatever happened to Big Mouth Moira who loved to talk and brag and pick on poor Truman? Well, she did not work in beauty salons like she had hoped. She ended up cleaning all of the dirty oil out of the Alaskan pipeline with a toothbrush.

DISMISSAL

The dismissal bell rang and another school day came to a close. The buses came, the children left, and Mrs. Frightenright was about to leave the classroom when the evil Principal Prickly-Pear walked into the classroom in his regular sneaky fashion. She knew that he was

always up to something, so she asked him, "Can I help you with something Principal Prickly-Pear?"

Principal Prickly-Pear looked around the room and said, "It has come to my attention, Mrs. Frightenright, that you are not being a good teacher!"

Mrs. Frightenright looked shocked! She asked, "How is it that I am not being a good teacher? My kids have some of the highest scores in this school!"

Principal Prickly-Pear had chosen to forget about that fact. He quickly changed the subject and his tone as he prepared to leave. "Oh, yes, well . . . um. I guess you are doing okay as a teacher, but I'm sure you will eventually do something wrong."

Principal Prickly-Pear left the room and slammed the door. Mrs. Frightenright just shook her head, thinking how peculiar he acted for a principal. She looked at her pocket calendar to see what was scheduled for Thursday. "Ah, yes, tomorrow I will bring my pet kangaroo into the classroom. The kids should just love my kangaroo!"

Beware, for tomorrow is
Thursday!

I wonder what will happen when Mrs. Frightenright brings her pet kangaroo into class. Here's a peek at some of the mischief that kangaroo will bring!

See **you** in class tomorrow!